When
the Soldiers
Were Gone

When the Soldiers Were Gone

VERA W. PROPP

SCHOLASTIC INC.
New York Toronto London Auckland Sydney
Mexico City New Delhi Hong Kong

ISBN 0-439-10402-5

Copyright © 1999 by Vera W. Propp.
Cover art © 1999 by Dan Andreasen.
All rights reserved. Published by Scholastic Inc.,
555 Broadway, New York, NY 10012,
by arrangement with G. P. Putnam's Sons,
a division of Penguin Putnam Books for Young Readers.
SCHOLASTIC and associated logos are trademarks
and/or registered trademarks of Scholastic Inc.

12 11 10 9 8 7 6 5 4   0 1 2 3 4 5/0

Printed in the U.S.A.   40

First Scholastic printing, January 2000

Book designed by Gunta Alexander. Text set in Goudy Old Style.

With thanks to the talented women of my
critique group, who always encouraged me and who
patiently listened as I read each chapter of this,
my first book, over and over again until I got it right:
Lynn Blankman, Patricia Gabree,
Caroline Petrequin and Margaret Watson.

With thanks to my husband, Richard,
for his constant support and encouragement.

With thanks to Refna Wilkin,
my editor at Putnam, who believed in this book.

With thanks to Sal Van Gelder.

Contents

1

Strangers

"Henk, come here!" Papa called. He did not sound happy. Henk wanted to go to him quickly, but Kootje's claws were caught in his sweater.

"Kootje, let go! Papa's calling. You know I can't take you in the front room," Henk said. One by one he got the kitten's little black claws out of his sweater.

"Down you go. I'll be right back." Henk gently put Kootje on the kitchen floor, patted the top of her head, and turned toward the door of the front room.

Papa's voice grew louder. "Henk, why don't you come? Can't you hear me calling you?"

What had he done wrong? Papa's gruff voice made Henk feel a little scared. "Here I come, Papa! Kootje was caught in my sweater."

"Leave Kootje. Come now!"

Henk opened the door just wide enough to squeeze through. He quickly closed it behind him so Kootje couldn't sneak by. But what was this? Papa wasn't alone. A man and a woman were sitting on the good sofa. They looked at Henk.

Henk slipped his hand into Papa's when he reached his side. He didn't take his eyes off the strange people on the sofa. They stood up. Oh, no! Were they coming over to him?

The man's clothes looked odd. He was wearing a dark suit, a white shirt and tie, and small leather shoes with laces. He was very thin. His suit looked much too big for him.

Here comes the woman! Her high heels clacked on the wooden floor. Mama never wore noisy shoes like that in the house. She always left her wooden shoes next to Papa's by the front door. She wore slippers when she was inside.

Henk hid his face behind Papa's leg. He was afraid the woman would try to kiss him. He only let Mama kiss him.

Papa's rough wool pants felt good against Henk's cheek. He would wear clothes just like Papa's one day.

He curled his arm around Papa's leg and pressed his face against it.

"Henk, let go of my leg, listen to me. I have something important to tell you," Papa said. His voice was soft and gentle again.

Henk didn't move. He didn't want to hear anything important from Papa in front of these people.

Then Henk felt strong hands on his shoulders turning his body away from Papa's leg. He had to look at the man and the woman again. Their skin was pale. Were they sick? Henk stared at their sad dark eyes.

"Henk, these people are your mother and father. Can you shake hands with them?"

No! Henk put his hands behind his back. Who did Papa say they were? Kootje was scratching at the door. Poor Kootje, Henk thought, she is lonely for me. He wanted to go to her. But what had Papa just said? The noisy scratching probably made him hear it wrong.

"What did you say, Papa?" Henk looked up at him.

Papa crouched down. Now Henk could look right into his eyes. Why did they look so wet? Papa cleared his throat. "Turn around, Henk, and meet your parents," Papa said.

Henk covered his ears. Papa pulled Henk's hands down and spoke again. His voice was husky. "Shake hands like I have taught you."

"No!" Henk cried, still looking into Papa's eyes. "You are my papa! Tell these people to go away!" He was shouting now.

Henk was hoping to see Papa's eyes crinkle up with laughter. This must be a joke. No. Papa's eyes stayed wide open and serious. Henk felt like bats were flying around in his stomach.

He turned and ran to the door, shouting as he ran, "NO, NO, NO! Tell them to go away. YOU are my papa! YOU are my papa! YOU are my papa! Kootje is my cat! Mama is my mama!"

He opened the door, scooped up Kootje, and held her close to his chest. He could hear Papa say, "It's my fault. I told him too suddenly." Henk slammed the door. Then he pressed his ear to the closed door.

The woman was crying. Papa was talking. "I tried to tell him many times during the past weeks that you were coming, who you were, who we were, but I couldn't," Papa said. "It never seemed the right time. I thought when he saw you he would remember you

4

and then it would be easier. I'm sorry, I've made it so difficult, and now we are all crying!"

Papa blew his nose.

Then the man said, "Don't blame yourself . . . after all you have done for us! We are alive today only because of you! After all, there is no easy way. I'm sure that when we are home and Benjamin has met his little brother, he will feel better."

The voices continued, but Henk didn't want to hear any more. He buried his face in Kootje's fur and sat down on the cushion in front of the fireplace. If only Mama were home, he thought.

He closed his eyes and tried to forget about everything that he had just heard. But questions kept lighting up inside his head like fireflies in a dark summer night. Why had Papa said that he had other parents? When had Papa tried to tell him this? Henk tried to remember. Why were these people here today? Why was everyone crying? Even Papa? Who was Benjamin?

It was quiet and warm in the kitchen in front of the fireplace. Kootje lay very still in Henk's arms. The only sounds were the kitten's purring and the crackling of the fire.

Time passed. Henk started to shiver. The fire had gone out, and Kootje's fur was cold and wet where Henk's face had been buried. Papa was sitting next to him in front of the fireplace. He took Henk's hand in his. "It's time for you to leave us, Henk," Papa whispered.

Good-bye

When Mama got home she had told Henk that Papa was right.

"Yes, Henk, they are your real parents. They love you and you must go with them," she had said.

Henk looked at her, still not believing what he heard. Her eyes were glistening just like Papa's. How could that be? How could he have other parents? Where would they take him? Who would take care of Kootje?

He stayed close to Mama as she busied herself in the kitchen. She tried to answer his questions. Finally he asked, "You love me, don't you?"

"I love you very much and I'll miss you very much,

Henk." Mama wiped her wet red eyes with the corner of her apron.

Then she bent down to hug Henk one more time. Her arms were soft and warm and smelled of soap. Henk hung on to her neck.

"They are waiting. You must go now." She pulled his arms down.

Mama took Henk's hand and walked with him out the front door. On the porch she kissed him on both cheeks. Henk tried to hug her again, but Mama stood up. She shook his hand formally, like they were playing a game. She pretended that she was saying goodbye to a very important person.

"Good-bye, Henk. Be a good boy," she said. "Don't forget us! We will always love you! I hope you will visit us very soon."

She bent down again and unwound Kootje from Henk's legs. She put the kitten in the house. Henk could hear her meows through the closed door. He covered his ears.

He wanted to run inside, grab Kootje, and hide under his bed. Would that make those people go away?

Papa came up the steps and took Henk's hand in his. "It's time," he said. They walked around the house toward the barn. In his other hand Papa held a suit-case. Under his arm was a small box tied with a blue ribbon.

Henk heard snorting and stamping hooves. He tightened his grip on Papa's hand as they rounded the corner of the house.

A large brown horse was hitched to a farm cart standing outside the open barn door. Henk sucked in his breath. Until this moment he had hoped it was all a big mistake. His eyes filled with tears.

The man who had been in the front room sat on the high seat of the cart. He was holding on to the horse's reins. Papa had said his name was David Van Sorg and his wife was Elsbet. She stood next to the cart. Henk looked down at the ground as he and Papa neared them. Papa put Henk's suitcase in the back of the cart. The man reached down and shook Papa's hand. "Thank you again," the man said. "We will never forget you!"

The woman shook hands with Papa, too, and she hugged him quickly. "Thank you," she said, wiping her eyes with a handkerchief. "Thank you." She climbed onto the cart and sat down beside the man.

Papa looked down at Henk and spoke in a hoarse

voice. "Don't cry, Henk. Be a big boy!" He bent over to hug Henk. Then, with a loud "ooopala," he lifted him onto the hay in back of the cart.

He handed Henk the small box tied with the blue ribbon. "This is from Miep and Pieter," Papa said. "They knew you would be leaving us but didn't know it would be today. The blue ribbon is from a dress Mama made for Miep's first birthday. Open the box when you get to your new home!" Henk dropped the box in back of him on the hay. He reached for Papa's hands again.

Papa leaned into the cart and kissed Henk. Henk tried to say something, but a large bubble of tears was stuck in his throat. Only his eyes could beg Papa to take him out of the cart. But Papa turned around and slowly walked away.

Memories

Hold on tight, Benjamin," the man said. He made a clicking sound and the cart started to move.

"My name is Henk," Henk mumbled, "not Benjamin."

Henk closed his eyes. He pretended he was riding around the farm in Papa's cart. The bumpy, swaying motion, the snorting of the horse, the dust from the road were just the same. But when he opened his eyes again he saw he was not in Papa's cart. He was in a different cart with a suitcase, a box with a blue ribbon, and his little wooden bed from the room he shared with Miep.

Henk saw the milk cows grazing in the fields. They didn't look up when the cart passed on the road. Yesterday he had been running after Pieter in the fields to bring the cows in. Today he was riding past the cows with two strangers who were taking him away from the home he loved. Would he ever be back?

Meneer Ten Eyck, the postman on his bicycle, waved. "Hallo, Henk!" he called. Henk felt too sad to answer. He looked away.

The woman turned around and looked at Henk. "Do you feel all right, Benjamin?" she asked. "Do you want to sit up here with us?"

"MY NAME IS HENK! MY NAME IS HENK!" he cried out loud. He turned toward the back of the cart. Tears welled up in his eyes again. Why didn't Papa say no to these people when they came to take him away?

When the cart passed the school Henk thought he might see his sister and brother, Miep and Pieter. He wanted to wave to them, to say good-bye, but no one looked out of the window.

Henk was old enough to go to school, too, but Papa hadn't sent him. He never told Henk why. Papa also never told Henk why only he had had to hide when the soldiers came.

Henk remembered that when the soldiers had

come to the farm during the war, everyone had been afraid. Usually a neighbor came to the door and whispered to Mama that the soldiers were coming. Mama's face turned white. Everyone started to talk in whispers, and Miep quickly moved the clothes hamper into the barn. Then she would help Henk climb into it.

"Be very quiet," she'd say. "Don't even sneeze!" She'd put the lid on and pile hay on top.

One day there had not been time to move the hamper into the barn. It had to stay in the kitchen with Henk inside. Miep had thrown dirty clothes on top to hide it. From inside the hamper Henk could see and hear the soldiers, but they couldn't see him.

They were very big and spoke to Papa in loud, gruff voices. One of them pointed a big gun at Papa. Two soldiers took Mama with them, stomping through the house and into the barn.

Miep sat at the kitchen table crying softly. Pieter sat on the floor staring at the soldier with the gun. Papa held his hands up high against the wall.

In the hamper Henk shut his eyes. He was too afraid to look anymore.

Finally he heard Mama and the soldiers come back to the kitchen. He opened his eyes again to see if

Mama was all right. One of the soldiers was carrying a basket filled with eggs and a sack with squawking chickens inside.

The soldiers stomped back to their truck and drove away. No one talked for a long time. Miep helped Henk out of the hamper and gave him a silver roll to play with.

After a while Mama said, "We all need a cup of tea."

It had been hard for Henk to stay quiet in the hamper, but he knew he had to do it. His legs ached and he was always afraid.

Sometimes the soldiers stayed so long that Henk fell asleep until Miep or Pieter shook the hamper to wake him up.

One time he had awakened by himself in the hamper. It was dark and cold. Where was he? Only the smell of the hay told him that he was in the barn. Henk couldn't see or hear anything—not even the cows. Where were the soldiers? He'd better be quiet.

What if the soldiers had taken everyone away with them? What would he do? Where would he go? Tears stung his eyes. He shivered. But he still didn't make a sound.

Finally Henk heard voices and footsteps and the mooing of cows. The barn door rattled open. The lamp was lit, and Miep helped Henk get out of the hamper. When they were back in the kitchen Mama held Henk on her lap. Papa started a fire in the fireplace and soon Henk felt warm again.

"The soldiers left the barn door open, Henk," Papa had explained, "and the cows were walking down the road. We all ran out so fast to bring the cows back that we forgot about you in the hamper! That will never happen again, Henk. I promise!" It never did.

Henk remembered when Uncle Jan had come to their house shouting, "It's over. The war is over! The Allied troops have come!"

Everyone laughed and danced around the kitchen. The next day Mama took the heavy curtains down from the windows. Papa, Pieter, Miep, and Henk went to the road to wave to the Allied soldiers when they marched by. These soldiers threw chocolate candy to all the children. Henk had never tasted anything so good!

The bad soldiers didn't come anymore after that. Henk often heard Mama singing in the kitchen and Papa whistling in the barn. He could run and play out in the fields with Miep and Pieter. The whole family had been happy, very happy.

Henk thought about all the sad and happy times on the farm while he rode along with the strangers. The cart passed places that Henk had never seen before. He didn't even know where he was going.

Could he run away from these people? Would Papa and Mama let Henk stay at home with them? How could he get back? Henk closed his eyes and tried to think of a plan.

4

Apelhem

Wake up, Benjamin!" Henk felt someone pulling on his shoulder.

Henk opened his eyes. Where was he? Who was this man? Who was Benjamin?

Henk stared at the man, then remembered. He was the pale man from the front room. He was calling *him* "Benjamin."

The man kept on talking. "We are home, we are in Apelhem!"

Henk knew about Apelhem, the city where Mama sold her eggs and chickens. But Apelhem was not *his* home.

The man helped Henk get out of the cart. He brushed the straw out of Henk's hair and off his clothes. Henk had never seen so many people in one place. Men in suits with ties and women in fancy dresses were everywhere. Young boys, dressed like him in short pants, walked in twos and threes down the sidewalks. But only Henk was wearing wooden shoes.

The man told Henk that the woman had gone into the bakery shop. They would stay outside with the horse. He held Henk's hand. Was he afraid Henk would run away? Henk looked up and down the busy street. Where would he run?

Three soldiers walked across the street toward them. Henk tightened his grip on the man's hand.

"You don't have to be afraid," the man said. "Those are the Allied soldiers. They are here to help us."

When the woman came out of the shop, she was carrying a package. "I got the last loaf of bread. It's good we stopped here first. Now let's hurry home."

They all got back into the cart. The man made the clicking sound and the horse started pulling the cart again.

What had happened to Apelhem? Many of the buildings were dirty; some had broken windows and large ragged holes in their brick walls. Pieces of glass and broken bricks lay piled up on the sidewalks. The horse had to move slowly to avoid large holes in the street.

"Do you remember hearing loud explosions when you were in the country, Benjamin?" the man asked.

Henk didn't answer.

The man continued. "Bombs were dropped on Apelhem from the Allied planes. The exploding bombs damaged the roads and buildings."

"If the Allies were good soldiers, why did they bomb Apelhem?" Henk asked.

"There were many Nazi soldiers here. The Allies bombed them and their gun factories, so they couldn't fight anymore. So they would go away."

"Soon Apelhem will look as beautiful as it did before the war," the woman added. "Many people still have no place to live because their houses were bombed. We were lucky. We found an apartment. As soon as we moved in, we came to get you so we could all be together again."

Henk wished that they hadn't found a place. Then he would still be with Mama and Papa. He turned to look out of the back of the cart again.

Many men and women were walking and riding bicycles.

At home only Meneer Ten Eyck had a bicycle. He used it to deliver the mail. The soldiers had taken everyone else's bicycles away. Henk remembered what Pieter had told him.

"Before the soldiers came, Henk, I had a shiny black bicycle." He had spread his hands wide, so Henk could see how big it was. "Papa taught me how to ride it and I rode it to school every day, with Miep sitting on back. Papa and Mama had bicycles, too. We all rode to church together. Mama's bicycle had a big basket on it to hold the eggs she sold in Apelhem. Some people tried to hide their bicycles from the soldiers, but we were afraid. 'We are strong enough to walk,' Papa had said. 'Better not make the soldiers angry.' "

So Pieter and Miep had walked a mile to school every day and Mama walked all the way to Apelhem when she had eggs to sell. But when the soldiers took the eggs, she didn't go to Apelhem at all.

These busy streets are very different from the dirt roads near the farm, thought Henk.

"Halt!" the man shouted to the horse as he pulled the reins.

The cart stopped in front of a tall brick building with many windows.

New Home

"We're home. This is where we live now, Benjamin. How do you like it?" the man asked. But he didn't wait for an answer.

He jumped down, helped the woman out of the cart, and then lifted Henk to the sidewalk. The man tied up the horse while the woman took a key out of her purse. She unlocked the big front door. This house had nothing broken, but why did it have to be locked up?

"This is your new home. Come, we have to go upstairs," the man said. Inside, Henk followed the man and woman up some steps. The woman took out another key and unlocked another door.

What kind of home was this, Henk wondered, that had to be locked by two keys?

They walked through the doorway into a large room. Boxes were piled in all the corners. The sun, streaming through the lace curtains, left a pattern on the bare floor. The only furniture was a small round table with four wooden chairs around it.

In one of the chairs a pretty lady sat with a baby on her lap. She stood up as the three of them walked into the room.

"Thank you, Katrina, for taking care of Carl today," the woman said. "Now I'd like you to meet our other son, Benjamin. He has been visiting our friends in the country."

Katrina shifted the baby to her left hip and shook hands with Henk. "Welcome home, Benjamin."

I'm not their son and this isn't my home, Henk wanted to say. And my name is HENK! But Papa had told him to be good. "Thank you," he mumbled without looking at her.

"Katrina, can you help me bring Benjamin's bed upstairs?" asked the man. "Then I will drive you home and return your father's cart to him."

"Of course," she said. She handed the baby over to the outstretched arms of the woman and walked out with the man.

"You are the big brother now. What do you think of Carl?" The woman held up the baby for Henk to see. "Isn't he a cute baby?"

Henk looked at the baby. He didn't know what to say. The baby didn't smell very good. Henk covered his nose and stepped back a little.

The woman nodded. "I'd better put a clean diaper on Carl now. Please take the loaf of bread to the kitchen. We will have something to eat soon. You must be hungry." She took the baby down a hall.

Henk did not feel hungry, but he thought he had better do what she asked. He carried the package of bread down the hallway to the kitchen. What a small room! Where was the fireplace? Henk put the bread on a small table and sat down next to it. The good smell of the warm bread reminded him of Mama.

He didn't like these streets filled with broken glass and holes. He didn't want to live in this house with the two keys. Would they lock him in? He had to find a way to get back home.

Henk heard the man and Katrina come back into the apartment with his bed. Where would Kootje sleep tonight? Tears came to Henk's eyes. He tried to wipe them away, but it was no use, they wouldn't stop. All of a sudden he remembered the box tied with the blue ribbon. "Oh, no!" he said. "How could I have forgotten it?" He wiped his eyes again and ran out of the kitchen.

Cake!

Henk went to the window in the front room to see if the cart with his box was still on the street below. No, the cart was gone, but he saw the man walking into the building.

As he waited at the window, another farm cart went by. If Papa would drive his cart to town, Henk thought, he would run down the steps and jump in beside him. Papa would take him home. He could forget all about these people and be with Kootje again! He'd look out of the window every day! Maybe Papa would come one day.

As soon as he heard the door open, Henk ran over to the man. "Where is my box?" he asked. "Papa gave me a box. It had a blue ribbon on it. It was in the cart! Where is the cart?" Henk spoke very quickly.

"Come, Benjamin, I'll show you." The man took Henk's hand and led him down the hall to a small room. There Henk saw his bed from the farm. The box with the blue ribbon and the suitcase were on it! The box wasn't lost! But still Henk felt sad. His bed didn't belong in this new room. He let go of the man's hand and walked slowly to the bed to open the box.

"You will sleep here, Benjamin," said the man. "And Carl will sleep over there in that little bed." He pointed to a crib.

Oh, no, thought Henk. I'll be sleeping in a room with a smelly baby!

"You two will become good friends when Carl gets a little older," said the man. Then he held out his hand. "Come, Benjamin, let's have some milk and cake. Your mother's friend Helga saved sugar for three months so she could bake a cake for your homecoming. Aren't we lucky?"

Cake! He'd open the box later! There was never cake at home. Mama said she didn't have sugar or butter to make cake. Even after the soldiers stopped coming, there was still no cake. When she had flour Mama baked bread. But Henk was sure that cake tasted better than bread. The books that Miep read to him showed pictures of happy children eating cake, sweet cake. Henk took the man's hand. Yes, he would go eat cake with these people!

The woman was in the kitchen. Carl lay on a blanket on the floor in the front room. Henk sat down next to the baby. Carl smelled better but he still didn't look happy. He just looked up at Henk with a serious face. Henk knew just what Carl was thinking because he was thinking the same thing: "Who are you?" He hoped that the baby wouldn't start to cry.

A whistle, like the sound from Mama's tea kettle, came from the kitchen. Henk felt sad as he thought about the big kitchen on the farm. He had been sitting in front of its warm fireplace with Kootje just that morning. The bats started flying around in his stomach again. Could he eat cake?

He saw that the table had been covered with a white cloth and set with three plates and three forks. There was a dark-brown cake in the middle of the table. A small glass of milk was by one of the plates. He sat there. The woman put a piece of cake on the plate in front of Henk. Oooh, it smelled good. He felt hungry! The bats were gone!

"Welcome home, Benjamin," the woman said, taking his hand. "Your father and I have talked about this moment over and over again. Now you are really here. We are very happy." Henk didn't say anything. He didn't feel happy or like he was at home. His home was on the farm.

Then the man spoke. "This sweet cake is a symbol of our sweet life together from now on. It looks good. Let's start."

While Carl played on the floor with a toy, the three of them ate cake. No one said any words . . . just "uummh, yum, yum, ummm!"

Henk ate slowly to make the cake last a long time. It *was* chocolate! It tasted just like the piece of candy a good soldier had given him after the war. He drank his milk in big gulps, while the man and woman sipped their hot tea slowly.

The woman then asked, "Do you like the cake, Benjamin?"

"Yes, thank you," he answered. He was getting used

to hearing that name, but he still wished they would call him Henk.

When his plate was empty, Henk looked at the rest of the cake still sitting in the middle of the table.

"No more today," the woman said. "Too much cake will make us sick. Our stomachs aren't used to sweets. Why don't you play with Carl, Benjamin, or read one of your old books." She pointed to an open box in the corner of the room, then she went into the kitchen. The man opened the newspaper.

Henk looked down at Carl. He was asleep on his blanket. Maybe one of the books would tell of children eating cake! That would be fun to read now that his stomach was full. Henk sat down on the floor next to the box of books. He began to take them out of the box, one by one. Would he be able to read them? Had Miep been a good teacher?

The Box with the Blue Ribbon

The first book Henk took out of the box had a picture of a skinny boy on the cover. He was dressed in short pants like Henk and had hair so curly it looked like a bush. The boy in the book was sticking out his tongue and wiggling his fingers in his ears. Henk knew this boy liked to cause a lot of trouble. I think I know his name, thought Henk. It's George, *George of the Rebel Club!* Henk opened the book to see if he could read it.

Yes! He *could* read most of the words! But why did the book have such a bad smell? He closed the book and started to take some of the other books out of the box. They all smelled the same.

The woman came over and sat next to Henk on the floor. "Do you remember *George of the Rebel Club,*

Benjamin? I read that book to you many times. You loved to hear about George."

She must have me mixed up with some other little boy, thought Henk.

The woman took more books out of the box. "Whew! These books smell terrible! They were in my friend Helga's cellar during the war." She took them all out of the musty box. "Let me hear you read, Benjamin."

Henk held his nose. He read a few short books to her. It was fun!

I wish Miep could hear me read, he thought. She would clap her hands. Maybe he would read to Carl someday. Maybe he could even teach Carl to read! Henk was *not* the baby now! He read the books from the box for the rest of the afternoon.

For supper they ate pea soup, bread, and cheese. Henk was very tired. After he had yawned for the third time, the man said, "Benjamin, I think it is time for you to go to bed."

"Your nightshirt is on your bed, Benjamin. We'll come in later to kiss you good night."

"I know how to go to bed by myself." He went over to the woman and shook her hand. "Good night," he said. Then he went to the man and did the same.

Henk went to his room. He sat on his bed and untied the blue ribbon and took the lid off the box.

Five silver rolls! Right on top! And a note from Pieter.

> *Dear Henk,*
>
> *I found these in the back field last March after the English planes flew over. I forgot all about them until yesterday. Now that the war is over there will be no more silver rolls, so I will give them to you as a present, little brother. Do you remember all the fun we had with them?*
>
> *Love, Pieter*

Henk ran his finger over the shiny little rolls. He remembered how the foil spirals sparkled in the sun when Pieter and he ran with them. Papa had explained to Henk that the rolls were dropped from planes so the planes would not be shot down. Henk didn't really understand this.

He put the silver rolls that Pieter had sent him under his pillow. If only Pieter were here to play with him.

Next Henk found a note from Miep on some pages torn from her notebook.

Dear Henk,

    Last week while you were out walking with Uncle Jan and Papa, I copied this story from one of my schoolbooks for you. I hope you will like reading it. I drew the pictures, too. Mama helped me a little bit. I hope you will come to see us.

Love, Miep

Henk was too tired to read the story. He put it under his pillow also. He'd read it the next day.

He looked back in the box and found a little wooden boat that he had seen Papa carving in the evenings. There was also a note from Papa.

Dear Henk,

    There is a little pond in the big park in Apelhem. You can float this boat there. Hold on tight to the string so it doesn't sail away from you! You are a good boy. I hope you can visit us soon.

Love, Papa

Henk thought he would rather float the boat on the pond at the farm. He put the boat under his bed.

One more thing was in the box, the sock doll that Mama made for Henk a long time ago. He had slept with it before he got Kootje. He kissed it and put it on his pillow.

As Henk lay very still in his bed, he heard Carl sucking his thumb. He heard other new sounds, too. Bicycle bells were ringing and people were walking and talking in the streets below his window. On the farm only the sounds of the animals in the barn, the crickets in the grass, and the wind blowing through the leaves had come into his room at night.

But sometimes on the farm, Henk had heard a truck rumbling down the road, and one time he had heard the truck stop right under his window, in front of the farmhouse. Then he had been afraid.

Scary Nights

"Help, help! I can't move my arms! Help!"

George, "the Rebel," was throwing a baby at Henk and his arms wouldn't move to catch it. The baby was falling, falling . . .

"Help! I can't catch it. He'll fall!"

A bright light . . . then voices. Where was he?

Henk opened his eyes, but they blinked closed again. In the two seconds of bright light he saw that he was not at home. He was in that new room, in that new house. He wasn't with Miep. He was with that baby. Could he move his arms? Yes! He opened his eyes again.

He had been dreaming.

The woman was standing by his bed. "Benjamin, what's the matter? Did you have a bad dream?"

The man stood right behind her. They both wore white nightclothes and looked like thin white ghosts with big, black eyes. Henk turned his head toward the wall.

The woman took his hand and continued talking softly. "You don't have to be afraid anymore, Benjamin. We are here and we will make sure that you are safe."

Henk remembered that on the farm he had often had bad dreams. When he woke up Miep would be standing by his bed. "Be very quiet," she would whisper. "Try to go back to sleep." Then she would lie down next to him in the dark room and he would feel safe. On the farm his dreams had often been about soldiers and guns and Papa with his hands up.

Sometimes he had been awakened during the night by Miep's screams. She had had bad dreams, too. Then Mama had come into the room. She sang a song to Miep very softly, but she never turned on the light.

The light was on in this room, and the man and the woman kept asking him questions. Henk decided not to tell them about his dream. He hadn't caught the baby when he was in danger. What would they think?

"I was dreaming about the soldiers," he lied.

"The soldiers are gone now, Benjamin," said the woman. "I dream of them, too. But when I wake up I remember that I don't have to be afraid anymore."

"We all still have bad dreams about the war," said the man. "But now that's all they are, bad dreams, not real life anymore!"

"Close your eyes, Benjamin. Try to go back to sleep. Do you want me to stay here with you?" the woman asked.

"No," Henk said, and closed his eyes. He wanted them to go away.

The woman kissed Henk on the cheek. The lights went out. He heard their slippers shuffle out the door.

The bright light in the room, just a minute before, reminded Henk of a very scary night on the farm. He had been in bed but not asleep yet. Miep had still been in the kitchen. He had heard a truck rumble to a stop outside his window. Oh, no, he had thought. Where can I hide?

Next he had heard a loud knock on the kitchen door below and the loud, gruff voices that always made him afraid. Then he heard the sound of heavy boots clumping up the stairs. Henk had held his breath. The footsteps got louder and louder as they came down the hall and then they stopped. Would they turn into his room? Yes. The light went on. Henk had squeezed his eyes shut. Maybe the soldiers will think I'm asleep, he had thought.

One soldier had stomped over to his bed. Henk could hear his breathing and smell the leather of his boots and the metal of his gun. Henk prayed silently, "Please don't hurt me."

Neither the soldier nor Henk moved for several minutes.

Finally the soldier grumbled to his partner, "Ach! There's just a baby here, no one else. Let's go, I'm tired!"

"Enough for tonight . . . you're right!" the other soldier answered from the far side of the room.

Then it was dark again. Henk didn't move while he listened to the sound of their boots tramping away from his room, down the hall, down the stairs. Again he heard their gruff voices in the kitchen and, finally, he heard the loud slam of the kitchen door.

Henk took a deep breath when he could no longer hear the rumble of their truck on the dirt road. Once again only the sounds of the wind in the trees and the animals in the barn filled the dark night outside.

He still remembered how he was shaking under his blanket when Papa came into the room a few minutes later.

"Everything is all right," Papa had said as he reached for Henk. But Henk could feel Papa shaking, too. Papa held him on his lap for a long time in that dark room.

Henk wondered if he would ever forget that scary night. He heard Carl breathing softly in his crib across the room.

Another Good Thing

When Henk woke up, the sun was shining through the window and the baby was crying. He heard the door open. Someone shuffled into the room. Henk pretended that he was still asleep. He could hear the woman talking to the baby. The crying stopped.

After the woman took Carl out of the room, Henk felt under his pillow for Pieter's silver rolls and Miep's story. They were still there. He read Miep's funny story about a bear who wanted to fly to the moon. He folded it up and put it back under his pillow. He would read it again later. He wished that he could fly to the moon or, better still, just back to the farm.

Henk got up and looked out of the window for Papa's cart. It wasn't there. Children with leather satchels on their backs were walking to school. A few looked about his age.

He was eight years old, but he had never been to school. Papa wouldn't let him go. "Mama needs you at home," Papa had said. "Pieter and Miep will teach you what they are learning in school. That will be good enough."

But Henk had always felt sad as he watched his brother and sister leave for school each morning.

If he could go to school, that would be another good thing about this place, besides the cake. What would the man and woman say if he asked them if he could go to school? He went down the hall to the front room.

"Good morning, Benjamin," said the man as he looked up at Henk from his newspaper.

"Good morning, Benjamin," said the woman. "Sit down. Here is some bread and cheese for your breakfast. Do you want milk?" Just then Carl threw his bowl of cereal on the floor!

"Oh, no," they all cried out together!

The woman wiped up the mess, then she went into the kitchen to get more cereal for Carl. She brought Henk a glass of milk.

Henk was afraid to ask the man about school while he was reading the newspaper. Suddenly the man folded the paper, picked up his hat, kissed everyone, and walked toward the door.

He's leaving, thought Henk. I missed my chance to ask about school. Now what should I do?

"Wish me luck with the lawyer," the man said to the woman as he opened the door. "I hope he will have good news!"

Then he looked right at Henk. "Benjamin, when I come home this afternoon we will go to the park. It is not far from here. And tomorrow morning we can walk to the school and find out when you can begin! Would you like that?"

Benjamin couldn't believe what he had just heard. "Yes," he said, "I would like to go to school."

"Then it's definite. I will take you tomorrow morning to sign up. Be a good boy. Good-bye." The man went out the door.

School! How had the man known what Henk was thinking? He would be going to school! Henk smiled and started to clap his hands but stopped himself. He had questions. Had Miep and Pieter taught him enough? Would the students laugh at him when he made a mistake? Would the teachers put him in kinder-garten with the babies? Maybe it would be better not to go to school.

"Now get dressed, Benjamin," the woman said. "We're going to the market to buy a chicken for our dinner. If we're too late, none will be left. After that, we'll buy you some new shoes. You can't go to school in wooden shoes!"

More Changes

After their long walk from the shoe store, the woman and Henk were eating lunch. Carl was taking a nap.

"You will not need to wear this anymore," the woman said softly. She opened the clasp of the silver chain around Henk's neck. It dropped into her hand with the little cross that had hung from it. She put them both in her apron pocket.

Henk grabbed his neck. "Why did you take my chain and cross? Mama told me it must stay on! What will Mama say? Is it not allowed to wear a chain to school either? Is that why you took it?"

The woman looked very serious. "No, that's not the reason, Benjamin. You probably don't remember when the chain was first put around your neck. It was a long time ago, but that cross on the chain saved your life!"

"What do you mean? How can a cross save a life? It's not not like a gun or a shield."

His neck felt bare.

"Will Miep take her chain with the cross off? Did it save her life, too?"

"No, Miep will not take her chain off. She is a Christian. The cross on the chain is a sign of her religion. But you are not Christian. You are Jewish like your father and me. Jewish people do not wear the sign of the Christian religion." The woman was holding his hand.

"But if I am not Christian, why was I wearing the cross?"

The woman paused then cleared her throat. "Mevrouw Staal, you call her Mama, put the cross on you when you went to live with her family. You had to look like a Christian Dutch boy. And they called you Henk, a common Dutch name."

"Henk is the name I like."

"I know," the woman said.

Her voice cracked as she continued. "If anyone heard you called Benjamin, your real name, they would have known that you were Jewish. Then bad things could have happened to you."

"But I was a good boy! Mama always said I was a good boy. What bad thing could happen to me?"

"Do you remember the soldiers who came to the farm sometimes?"

"Oh, yes. I remember the soldiers. Everyone was afraid when they came! They had guns and they stomped through our house. I had to hide in the clothes hamper when they came!"

"That's because they were looking for Jewish children like you." She took a deep breath. "If they found them, they took them away."

Henk put his knife and fork down. "I didn't know the soldiers wanted to take me. Why didn't Papa tell me?"

"You were a little boy, Benjamin. He didn't want to frighten you any more than he had to. He told us you were very good. You always obeyed him when he told you to hide and be quiet."

"I hated being in that hamper. It was so small that I couldn't move. But Papa should have told me! I almost sneezed sometimes. Then the soldiers would have found me. I'm glad they never did."

The woman's voice became a little hoarse. "But what if the soldiers had rushed into the house before you could jump into the hamper? It was important that you wore the cross in case that happened. If the soldiers thought that they had found a Jewish child, you and the whole Staal family would have been arrested, maybe killed."

That's why Papa sometimes looked at me with such a sad face, Henk thought. Everyone in the family was in danger because of me.

He wanted to go to the window to look for Papa, but the woman started talking again softly. "Mevrouw Staal told me that one time the soldiers came in the night. They marched right into your room. When they saw you asleep with the cross around your neck, they left you alone."

Henk shivered. "I remember that night." He leaned over and whispered, "I only pretended to be asleep. Maybe I still need the cross to guard me."

"No, Benjamin. Thank God, the soldiers are gone. You are safe with your father and me now. No one will hurt you."

"But where are they? Where did they come from? How do you know they won't be back?"

Just then the door opened and the man walked in. He kissed the woman and Henk and sat down to have lunch.

"You look quite handsome in your new sandals, Benjamin. How do they feel?" he asked.

"All right," Henk said politely.

"They're probably still a little uncomfortable, aren't they?"

"They're not too bad," Henk said. "But I tripped three times walking home from the store! Can I still wear my wooden shoes sometimes?"

The man smiled at Henk. "Of course you can! When we go out to the country!"

When will that be, Henk thought? Soon, he hoped. Maybe they would let him stay there. Or . . . maybe he could hide so the man and woman would have to return to Apelhem without him.

The woman brought out the cake from yesterday and they each ate another piece. It still tasted delicious.

"Now tell me about your meeting this morning, David," the woman said to the man.

While the adults talked, Henk went over to the window and looked out. His hand went up to his bare neck. Was he really safe now? How could he be sure?

Danger in the Park?

The man and the woman are always very kind to me, Henk thought, as he looked out the window. But they are *not* Mama and Papa!

Henk knew their names were Elsbet and David. It wouldn't be proper to call them by their first names. What should I call them, he asked himself? How do I know if they are really my parents as they say they are?

Henk walked across the room and sat on a box. He watched Carl suck on his bottle. The baby looked happy on Elsbet's lap. What would this baby say to him if he could talk?

Later, Elsbet got Carl ready for their walk to the park. David and Elsbet carried the carriage down the steps, and Henk trailed after them.

Henk lifted his feet in his new sandals slowly and carefully, so he wouldn't stumble as he walked. What was that music he heard? It sounded like happy, tinkly music, but as it got louder and louder, the bats started flying around in his stomach again. He didn't want to hear the music. But why? He wanted to go back to the apartment. Henk looked at Elsbet and David. They didn't look afraid.

They all walked on.

Soon Henk saw a large gate. An old man there was turning a handle on a big red and gold box. The tinkly tunes came right out of that box. A cute little monkey on a string danced around the gate. The monkey held out a tin cup to the people there.

The music was too loud! Henk put his hand over his mouth. He hoped he wouldn't get sick.

Through the park gate Henk saw grass and flowers and trees. He saw mothers sitting on white benches with babies on their laps. He saw children playing with balls and kites. He could hear their shouts and laughter.

His heart started to beat fast. He had to get away from this place!

When David let go of his hand to put a coin in the

monkey's cup. Henk whipped around and started to run away from the park gate as fast as he could.

But he had forgotten that he was wearing those new sandals. An uneven edge of the sidewalk caught one foot and a second later he was flat on the sidewalk. His knees hurt. His stomach hurt. His heart seemed to be beating in his throat. He was crying and he was scared.

"Benjamin, what's the matter?" David and Elsbet had caught up to him. They helped him stand up.

"I can't be here! I can't play here." These words tumbled out of Henk's mouth. "Take me home!"

"Of course you can play here," said David. "That's why we came to the park on this nice day."

"No, I can't play in the park. I'm afraid! The man with the gun will see me!"

The Man with the Gun

Henk cried all the way home. But he stopped shaking as soon as the door to the apartment closed behind him.

Elsbet washed the blood from Henk's knees. She wiped the tears off his cheeks. She helped Henk into his nightshirt.

"I don't want to go to that park ever again! The music made me feel sick," Henk told her.

"Do you know why it made you feel bad?" Elsbet asked.

"It made me think of a big man. He wouldn't let me play in the park with my friends. He had his hand on a gun. He yelled at me to go home. Was I dreaming again?"

"No, Benjamin, it really happened. It happened a long time ago."

Elsbet and Henk sat down on the side of his bed. She kissed his hand and held it next to her cheek. Then she looked into his eyes. She talked to him softly.

"One day you and I were walking home from my friend's house. You heard the music from the organ grinder as we got near the park gate. You ran ahead to watch the monkey. You had done that many times before."

Henk picked up his sock doll and held it close to his chest.

Elsbet continued. "When I got to the gate I saw a big sign that had not been there before. The sign said that Jewish people were not allowed to go into the park anymore. Then I saw a soldier clutching your arm. I ran to you. He was asking you many questions—your name, where you lived, who your parents were. But you didn't answer him. I think you were too afraid. Then he ordered you to stay away from the park."

"He had hidden behind the gate," Henk said. "I was scared when he jumped out and grabbed me."

"The other children in the park had been running around making a lot of noise. But when they saw the soldier, they stopped playing. They watched as he held you. They listened as the soldier told you that he would always be there to make sure you did not sneak into the park. The children did not make a sound."

"Were they afraid, too?"

"Oh, yes. Everyone was afraid of the soldiers."

"Why did the soldier let all the other children play? How did he know I was Jewish?"

"I'll show you," Elsbet got up and went out of the room. When she returned she was holding a small blue wool coat. A yellow star was sewn on its front.

Henk jumped off the bed and grabbed the coat from her. He sniffed it. He knew the smell of this coat. He rubbed his hand over the collar and sleeves. He knew the way its wool cloth felt. He laid it down on the bed and traced the outline of the yellow star with his finger. He remembered that he had traced a yellow star like this before.

Elsbet watched him without speaking.

Finally, Henk held the coat up to his chest. It did not even cover his short pants and the sleeves came only to his elbows. It was a coat for a very small boy. "I think this is my coat," he said.

"Yes," said Elsbet, "it is your coat. The soldier in

the park saw the yellow star on the coat. That's how he knew you were Jewish." She spoke very softly. "Everyone who was Jewish had to wear a yellow star. It was the law. And new laws for Jews were made every week."

Her voice became almost a whisper, and she took both of Henk's hands into hers. "Jews couldn't own cars or bicycles. We couldn't ride buses either. We walked everywhere. We couldn't go into certain stores. Jewish children couldn't go to public schools or use libraries."

"Jewish children couldn't play in the park," Henk added.

"And they couldn't swim in the public pools," Elsbet continued. "Jewish men and women lost their jobs. Those were bad times, Benjamin."

Henk could see tears in Elsbet's eyes. She wiped her cheek. "When I took your hand, the soldier let go of your arm. Then you and I walked home. You were shaking all over, but I couldn't find the words to explain what had happened. You were so little."

"I don't remember walking home."

"We never went near that park again until today. David and I thought you would be happy to go there and play. We didn't know you would remember that terrible day so long ago."

"I didn't remember it until I heard that music! Are you sure that soldier isn't still there?"

"Yes, I'm sure, Benjamin," she said. "All the bad soldiers are gone; they will not be back. Everyone can play in the park now."

An Enemy in School

Henk felt excited when he woke up the next morning. At last he would go to school. He tried not to think about the park.

But as he walked to school holding David's hand, he started to worry. Would the teachers tell him he couldn't go to school? Was he smart enough? Did he look all right? Could they tell that this was his first day in sandals?

Everything went very fast. They went to the principal's office and David signed some papers. The principal asked Henk some arithmetic questions and gave him a story to read out loud.

Then the principal took Henk down a long hall and into a classroom. He introduced him to the teacher.

The children stared at him. They didn't look very friendly. The teacher talked to the principal and David. She didn't see one of the boys put his fingers in his ears and wiggle them at Henk. He stuck his tongue out, too. Just like George in *George of the Rebel Club*, thought Henk, but it didn't seem funny like in the book. Once more the bats started flying in his stomach.

"Be good and listen to the teacher, Benjamin!" David said as he left the classroom.

The teacher smiled at Henk and handed him two books. Then she pointed to an empty desk. Oh, no, thought Henk, the desk was right next to the boy who had made a face at him.

The boy stared at Henk but didn't speak. Henk slid into the seat and put the books and his new notebook and pencils inside the desk. Then he looked around the room.

The teacher had blonde hair and was wearing a white blouse. She looked pretty, Henk thought. Would she be nice?

A large chalkboard was in front of the room. Henk recognized Queen Wilhelmina's picture above the chalkboard. A Dutch flag hung in the corner of the room.

Most of the other children were chatting and laughing. Some were reading or drawing. One or two looked at him, but no one talked to him. Would any one of them ever be his friend?

A loud bell rang. The noise stopped. The students turned to face the front of the room. They clasped their hands in front of them on their desktops. No one moved, no one talked.

Henk brought his hands from his lap to his desktop.

All eyes were on the teacher. She stood and looked up and down the rows of faces in front of her. She stared at one girl. The girl quickly took something out of her mouth. She stared at a boy. He sat up straighter.

Finally the teacher smiled and said, "Good morning, class."

"Good morning, Mejuffrouw Ten Broek," the students responded in a singsongy way.

"Today we welcome your new classmate, Benjamin Van Sorg." She looked at Benjamin. "Benjamin, please stand."

Henk stood by his desk. His face felt very hot. He still felt like "Henk" but no one at school would know that name. He had to be "Benjamin" now.

"Welcome, Benjamin." The students used the same singsongy rhythm as before.

Henk sat down quickly.

"Take out your arithmetic books, class. Turn to page 43," the teacher said. "Willem van den Bosch, come to the chalkboard and show the class how you solved problem number 3."

A boy two rows over stood up, walked to the front of the room, and wrote a multiplication problem on the chalkboard. Henk watched him closely. He remembered the evenings he had sat with Pieter and Miep at the big kitchen table on the farm while they did their homework. Pieter had taught him how to multiply.

Henk smiled as he watched the numbers appear on the chalkboard. "I can do that!" he said to himself.

The second boy who went to the chalkboard made a mistake. The teacher told him to sit down and asked another student to go correct the error. Henk noticed that the boy next to him had stuck his foot in the aisle.

The boy who had made the mistake would trip on it going back to his seat. Should he warn him? How?

Henk looked up into the boy's eyes, then down toward the floor. The boy looked down, too, and saw the foot just in time to step over it. He stuck his tongue out at Henk's neighbor.

At the end of the arithmetic lesson the teacher said, "Tonight you must do the problems on page 45. Now take out your history books. Jan Doorn, start reading to the class on page 101."

Henk opened his other book. He read the words on the page silently along with the boy reading out loud.

Then he heard, "Continue, Benjamin Van Sorg."

Oh, no!

Henk could feel the eyes of every student in the room on him. He slowly slid out of his seat and stood. His face got hot again.

The room grew quiet. Henk cleared his throat and read to the end of the page. Then the teacher thanked him and asked the next student to read. Henk took a deep breath and slid back into the safety of his seat.

When it was time to go home for lunch, Elsbet and

Carl were waiting for him. Henk pushed Carl's carriage for a little while. Then he ran ahead, happy to stretch his legs.

After lunch Elsbet let Henk walk the three blocks back to school by himself. In the afternoon the students studied geography and science.

When the final bell rang, Henk couldn't wait to be out of the stuffy school. He would run all the way to the apartment.

Outside Henk sucked in a big breath of fresh air. Whew! That felt great. It made him happy to hear the *brüings* of bicycle bells and the chattering of the students. He hadn't known school would be so quiet.

Henk hopped on one foot down the six steps to the sidewalk. He held his new geography book in one hand and his notebook in the other. Hopping will be easier when my books are in a satchel on my back, he thought.

Many of the students were getting on bicycles, but some were walking home. At the curb he stood and watched the bicycles pass by. The boy who sat next to him was holding his hand up as he was riding past. Was he waving?

Henk started to wave back, but saw that the boy had something in his hand. What was he shouting?

Henk felt a sharp pain on his forehead. Tears came to his eyes as his hand flew up to the place that hurt. It felt rough and wet. When he looked at his hand, it was covered with bright red blood. He tried to wipe the blood from his forehead with his hand, but there was too much.

"Max shouldn't have done that!" Another boy from his class had come over to Henk. "Here, take my handkerchief. You can bring it back to me tomorrow." The boy started to walk away.

"Wait a minute." Henk held the handkerchief to his forehead. "Did you hear what that boy yelled at me? What did he say?"

"Of course I heard. Are you deaf? He yelled 'dirty Jew.' Max hates Jews!" The boy hurried off down the sidewalk.

Henk continued on his way home. His head ached. He didn't feel like running anymore.

14

Still Afraid

Elsbet washed the cut on Henk's forehead and put a large bandage on it. She leaned over to kiss him, but Henk turned his face away.

"Does your forehead hurt a lot?" she asked, taking his hand in hers.

"My whole head hurts!"

"You had better rest for a while. I'll bring you some books to read." Elsbet left the room. She returned with two books from the box in the front room. Henk didn't want to read those books. He left them on the table by his bed. He reached under his pillow and took out Miep's story from the box with the blue ribbon.

Elsbet left the room with the bloody handkerchief. David came in a little later with a shiny brown leather satchel. "I carried a satchel just like this one when I went to school," he said as he handed it to Henk. "This is for you." Then he gently peeled back the bandage to examine Henk's cut.

"I'm sorry this happened to you, Benjamin," he said softly, replacing the bandage.

Henk put the satchel on the floor. "Do I have to go back to school?" he asked. "I could learn at home like I did on the farm. No one likes me at school."

"There are some mean people everywhere, Benjamin, but there are nice ones, too, like the boy who gave you the handkerchief. Do you know the name of the boy who threw the stone?"

"His name is Max. He sits right next to me."

"Do you want me to talk to the teacher about him?"

"No! Just let me go back to the farm."

"This is your home now, Benjamin. Try again at school tomorrow. I'm sure it will be better." David sat down beside him. "During the war many people said bad things about Jews. Some people still believe they are true."

"No one was mean to me on the farm."

"Benjamin, all the people of Holland suffered during the years when the Nazi soldiers ruled our country. When people don't have enough to eat, they want to blame someone. The Nazis told the Dutch people that the Jews were the cause of everything bad that happened to them."

"Is that true?"

"No, of course not! Jews were hungry, too, but also we were always in danger."

"But you told me that I didn't have to be afraid anymore. I'm afraid of Max!"

"The Nazi soldiers are gone, Benjamin. Now the school will not allow Max to hurt you. Try again tomorrow. You will find some friends there, too. You'll see."

"I bet I could hit Max with a stone when he rides past me on his bicycle tomorrow. Then he'll leave me alone."

"Benjamin, promise me that you will not throw a stone at Max. You are in school to learn, not to fight. If he behaves badly you must tell the teacher. Do you promise?"

Henk thought about the pretty blonde teacher. "Yes, I promise," he said.

He remembered how angry Max's face had looked when his hand was raised with the stone. He also remembered how often he had wished he could go to school. He didn't know then that it would make him afraid.

A Friend at Last

The next morning Henk combed his hair over his forehead and wore a hat to school hoping to hide the bandage. Of course, he had to take off the hat when he entered the classroom. He was sure all the students were staring at his forehead.

Max's seat was still empty. The boy who had given him the handkerchief walked over to Henk's desk. "How does your head feel?" he asked.

"It doesn't hurt anymore, but I have to keep the cut covered up. I wish the other students wouldn't look at it. Do they know what happened?" Henk handed the boy the washed handkerchief.

"Oh, yes. Most of them saw Max throw the stone. They expected trouble from him, but I think everyone was surprised that it would be on your first day! Thanks for warning me about his foot in the aisle. I think he was hoping that I would fall and he could blame it on you."

"Why does he want to get me in trouble?"

"Here he comes! I'll tell you at lunchtime. Wait for me outside." The boy went quickly to his own desk and slid into the seat.

Max had a big smile on his face as he looked at Henk's forehead. He sat down and stuffed his books into his desk. Henk kept his eyes on the front of the room.

The morning went by quickly. They studied arithmetic and history just like the day before.

At lunchtime the boy was waiting for Henk on the front steps of the school. As they walked down the sidewalk together he told Henk that his name was Jop Older.

"Most of the students hate Max," said Jop. "We try to stay out of his way."

"Has he ever thrown a stone at you?"

"No. He threw it at you because you're Jewish. He hates Jews."

"But how did he know I was Jewish? I wasn't wearing a yellow star on my clothes."

"Max's father is a policeman. He was a member of the Green Police during the war."

"Who are they?" asked Henk.

"The Green Police are the Dutch policemen who helped the German Nazis find Jews in Holland. Max told his father your name when he went home for lunch yesterday. His father told Max that your family is Jewish. After lunch Max told everybody."

"I wish that I didn't have to go to this school. How can I keep out of Max's way? I sit right next to him."

"When Mejuffrouw Ten Broek hears what happened, she'll probably move you to a different desk. But don't worry, he can't do much in the classroom." Jop stopped walking. "I have to turn here. Good-bye."

Jop took a few steps then stopped and shouted to Henk, "Willem and I are going to the park after school today to fly our kites. Ask your mother if you can come with us."

"Will Max be there?"

"I don't think so."

"Well, then I will," Henk shouted back. He ran the rest of the way to the apartment.

16

Oh, No! Max Again!

Henk hardly noticed the music as he walked toward the park gate with Willem and Jop that afternoon. They were arguing about whose kite could fly higher. Henk was looking for Max.

It was warm and breezy—a perfect day for flying kites. Henk saw triangles of every color and size inside the park gates. Some were already in the sky. Was every child in Apelhem flying kites? He did not see Max.

"Here I go," said Willem, "watch 'Big Blue' go up!" He ran across the grass, holding his kite as high as he could so it could catch a breeze.

Henk sat on the grass watching Willem and helping Jop untangle the string of his kite. "It's up! Look, Jop!"

Willem's kite was flying high over the park. Willem was standing on the other side of the field. He was looking up and holding tight to what was left of his ball of string.

Soon Jop's kite was in the air, too. Jop and Henk took turns holding its string as the breezes blew it higher and higher.

It was a wonderful afternoon.

When Willem's kite was blown into the branches of a tree, Henk scrambled up the tree and got it loose. He had climbed many trees on the farm!

"Thanks, Benjamin," said Willem. "How did you get up there so fast?" He ran down the field again, his kite held high.

Henk was straddling a big branch. He was halfway up the tree and could look over the whole park. He watched Willem and Jop and the other kite-flying children run up and down the field. Then he saw Max.

Max was riding his bicycle on the other side of the field. What should he do? Would Max come near? Should he hide up in the tree? He watched Max circling the field. The bicycle path went right under the branches of his tree. Henk's fingers went up to the bandage on his forehead.

Jop called to him, "Benjamin, come down. It's your turn to fly the kite."

"Here I come," Henk yelled back to him.

When he looked down he saw that Max was close, but he thought he could get to the field before Max got to the tree. I don't have to hide from him, thought Henk. He climbed down to a lower branch, then jumped to the ground.

Henk landed right in front of Max's bicycle! Had Max speeded up?

"Watch out!" Max yelled. He stomped on his brakes hard. The bicycle skidded to a stop and Max fell off. His bicycle landed on top of him.

Henk froze. Now what would Max do to him?

Jop had seen the whole thing from the field and was calling to Henk again. "Come here, Benjamin, quick!"

Henk looked over at Jop, then again at Max. He couldn't run away. He didn't want Max to think he was a coward. Maybe Max was hurt badly.

Max got up off the ground slowly. He glared at Henk. "So it was the dirty Jew who made me fall. Wait till I tell my father!"

Henk was shaking. "Tell him! All I did was jump

out of a tree. You're right, I am Jewish, but I'm *not* dirty! I take a bath every day. Look at you."

Max tried to brush the dust from the path off his clothes. He took a step toward Henk. His fists were clenched. His face was red. Then he stopped. "Wait till I tell my father!" he said again. He turned, stepped back, and picked up his bicycle.

Henk ran toward Jop. "Here I come. Is it my turn?"

17

Papa!

Henk's days became busy with school and his new friends, Jop and Willem. Mejuffrouw Ten Broek did change Henk's desk, and he stayed away from Max when they were not in the classroom. No one mentioned the accident in the park.

Henk walked with Jop and Willem to school every day, and they often went to the park after school. They flew their kites or sailed the wooden boat that Papa had made. Once Henk brought the silver rolls that Pieter had sent in the box with the blue ribbon. The three boys threw the rolls at each other, watching them sparkle in the sun as they unwound.

When he was walking to school or to the park, Henk always looked for Papa and his cart.

One day Elsbet asked him to come home early from the park. She wanted him to play with Carl while a friend was visiting her.

Henk shouted "good-bye" to his friends as he ran through the big gate. He stopped at the curb to look up and down the street to see if it was safe to cross. At the very end of the street he saw a farm cart. It was Papa!

"Papa," Henk yelled, "Papa, wait!"

He ran down the street, following the cart. By the time he got to the corner the cart was gone. It had turned the corner. Now it was going down the new street. Henk could still see it. He ran after the cart again, yelling, "Papa, stop! It's me—Henk! Stop!" It turned again. So did Henk. Then it turned onto a very wide, busy street. The cart moved slowly because students bicycling home were in the way. Then a policeman stopped the cart at a busy corner so traffic could pass. Henk caught up to it. His breath was coming in gasps after running for so many blocks.

"Papa!" he yelled. "Papa, it's me—Henk!"

He put one foot up to climb into the cart. Papa would be happy to see him! He looked up at the driver.

It *wasn't* Papa!

The driver was a farmer. He was dressed like Papa, in a dark shirt and heavy pants, but it wasn't Papa!

"Excuse me, Meneer. I made a mistake," Henk said to the man up on the seat. He stepped down quickly and stood on the sidewalk. He watched the policeman wave the cart on. He felt like crying.

How could he have been so wrong? Had he forgotten what Papa looked like already? Henk sat down on a bench to catch his breath. Why didn't Papa ever come to Apelhem? If the man had been Papa, could Henk have gone back to the farm with him? Did he want to?

He was getting used to living in Apelhem. He didn't even sleep with Mama's sock doll anymore, but at night he still missed Kootje in his bed.

School was not as much fun as he had thought it would be. But he had two friends there. He also had one enemy!

Elsbet and David were good to him. He even liked playing with Carl sometimes.

Carl! He had forgotten! Elsbet wanted him home early to play with Carl! He had promised he would be home early.

Henk looked around. He didn't know where he

was. Nothing looked familiar. He jumped up from the bench and started to walk. He didn't remember how many turns he had made. He had just been following the cart and thinking about Papa. No. This street didn't look right. He turned around and started the other way. Where was the park? He knew his way home from the park. He turned a corner. Still nothing looked familiar.

It was no use. He was lost. He was also very late. What would Elsbet say?

He went back to the bench. The policeman who had been directing traffic on the busy corner was sitting there reading a newspaper. Should he ask the policeman for help? What if he was Max's father? He had to take a chance.

"Excuse me, Meneer. I think I'm lost," Henk said politely to the policeman on the bench. "Can you tell me how to get to the big gate at the park?"

"Of course," said the policeman, "I have to go by there on my way home." He folded his newspaper and got up. "Come with me."

The policeman asked Henk how he had gotten lost.

"I just got mixed up," Henk said.

"You better pay attention when you are walking by yourself!" the policeman warned.

Soon they heard the music of the organ grinder. When they got to the gate, Elsbet was just crossing the street, pushing the baby carriage.

"Benjamin, where have you been? Are you all right? Did you forget that I needed you this afternoon?" She talked very fast.

The policeman told her where Henk had been. "Maybe he is too young to be walking by himself," the policeman said. Elsbet thanked him, and the policeman continued on his way. Then Henk had to tell her about his big mistake.

"Don't ever run off again, Benjamin. I was very worried about you. We will go to visit the farm one day very soon. Promise me that you will only walk to the school or the park by yourself, nowhere else!"

"I promise. I'm sorry that I made you worry."

"When you are older you can go other places, too. But I have to know that you can find your way home first. I worried about you all the time we were apart during the war. I don't want to start worrying about you again!"

18

We Had to Hide

At the apartment Elsbet brought out an old, crinkled photograph. She sat down at the table where Henk had already started his homework.

"What's that?" he asked her.

"This is the photograph that kept me alive during the war, Benjamin," she said. She flattened it out on the table.

"I had this photo with me always. I kept it in a bag I wore next to my heart." She handed it to Henk.

He studied it for a minute. "That's me!" he exclaimed. "That's a picture of me! But I look like a baby!"

"Yes, Benjamin, it's you. I kissed this photo every

morning and every night. Not being with you was the worst thing that happened to me during the war. I thought about you every minute of every day."

"Then why did you send me away?"

Elsbet took a deep breath. "Your father explained to you last week that the soldiers we were all afraid of were called Nazis. Do you remember?"

"Yes," Henk said. He put down his pencil. "He told me that Germany's ruler was a bad man and he wanted to rule Holland, too. The Nazis were his soldiers."

"That's right. His name was Adolf Hitler, and he also wanted to get rid of all the Jewish people in Germany and Holland," Elsbet went on.

"But why?"

"He gave many reasons, Benjamin, but they were not good reasons. You'll learn about them when you are a little older."

"He wouldn't let me play in the park. That was mean," Henk said.

"Hitler wanted to make life very hard for Jews, so that we would leave Holland. But there was no place to go," Elsbet said. "Besides, Holland was our home, Benjamin."

"But why couldn't the Dutch people just tell the German soldiers to go home? Why didn't they fight them?"

"The German army was too powerful. The Dutch people had no choice. They had to obey Hitler to stay alive," Elsbet said.

"Were the soldiers that came to Papa's farm his soldiers?"

"Yes, Benjamin. Many of them were German soldiers. But many were Dutch, too. They were all called Nazis. Hitler ordered the Nazi soldiers to go to every house where they thought Jewish people lived and arrest them. They took Jewish men, women, and children away on trucks."

"I saw their trucks sometimes."

"Then they forced the Jewish people to get onto trains that took them to work camps. Many died in these camps from sickness and starvation. Some were killed . . . like Carl's mother and father."

"What?" Henk looked down at Carl playing on a blanket next to the table. "I thought *you* were Carl's mother."

"Carl is my sister's baby, Benjamin. The Red Cross found him in one of the work camps after the war.

His mother, my sister, Debora, had died there. They couldn't find his father, but they found me and brought him to me. Carl will always be like my own son, just like you." Elsbet leaned over and picked up the baby.

Henk watched her tickle Carl. The baby giggled. Maybe he doesn't laugh much because he misses his mother and father, Henk thought. He knew how that felt.

"Many Jews hid so they wouldn't be sent to these death camps and many Christians helped them," she continued. "Your father and I decided that the best chance we had to stay alive would be to go into hiding also. But it would be very difficult to find a safe place. We knew that a little boy, like you, could not hide with us."

"I am good at hiding," Henk whispered.

"Yes, I know you had to learn that." She picked up the photograph again, then continued. "When Paul Staal and his wife offered to let you live on their farm, we said yes. They had brought fresh farm eggs to your grandfather's grocery store for many years. We knew they were good people. Meneer Staal drove into Apel-hem to deliver eggs the next week and we put you and your bed in the back of his cart on the straw. We told you that you were going for a visit to a farm. Miep came with her father that day to play with you in the cart, so you wouldn't be afraid."

Henk remembered that Miep knew a lot of games.

"Soon you forgot you had other parents. You thought the Staals were your mama and papa. That was good. If anyone asked you any questions, you couldn't give us away."

"Where did you go? Did you live on a farm, too?"

"We lived on many farms, Benjamin. We hid in dark attics or in the woods or in very damp cellars. When a farmer thought that someone knew he was hiding Jews, he became afraid. Then we had to leave his farm in the middle of the night. We had to find another hiding place. Some days we had nothing to eat. We were always in danger. We prayed every day that the terrible war would end. Then we would be safe and we could all be together again."

The Sabbath

Henk went to school every day, David went to his job at the bank, and Elsbet took care of Carl at home. Henk had been living with David and Elsbet for six weeks. He had learned that Fridays and Saturdays were special days in their home.

On Fridays Elsbet went to the butcher shop even before Henk left for school. She always bought a chicken for the Sabbath eve dinner.

When Henk came home from school on Friday afternoons he could smell the chicken roasting. Then he flew up the stairs, two steps at a time. He didn't stop until he reached the warm oven door!

"Be careful! You'll burn yourself," Elsbet always warned. She would be at the kitchen table, polishing the silver candlesticks or chopping vegetables. Carl was usually in his high chair eating.

"Have something to eat, Benjamin," Elsbet said, "then play with Carl in the front room. I have to peel the potatoes. Later you can help me set the table."

David always came home early from his job at the bank on Fridays. He would take Carl on his knee and play horsey. Then Henk could help Elsbet.

Henk placed the silver candlesticks, the wine cup, and the plate for the challah, the braided Sabbath bread, at their special places on the good tablecloth.

At sunset Elsbet lit and blessed the Sabbath candles and called Henk, Carl, and David to the table.

בָּרוּךְ אַתָּה יְיָ אֱל הֵנוּ מֶלֶךְ הָעוֹלָם,
שֶׁהֶחֱיָנוּ וְקִיְּמָנוּ וְהִגִּיעָנוּ לַזְּמַן הַזֶּה.

Blessed are You Lord, our God, Ruler of the universe, for giving us life, for sustaining us, and for enabling us to reach this happy day.

The four of them always held hands while David and Elsbet said this prayer. They also said a special prayer for Carl's mother and father and all the others who had died during the war. Then they blessed the bread and wine. Finally, they ate the chicken dinner!

"We can never forget our terrible years during the war when we were apart from you, Benjamin," David reminded Henk, "and we must always remember to thank God that we are together again."

"Soon we will move back into our house, Benjamin. From there you will be able to walk to the synagogue after school to learn Hebrew. Then you will be able to say the prayers with us," Elsbet said.

"Why don't we live there now?" Henk asked.

"After we left the house to go into hiding, German officers moved in," David answered. "We'll visit the house one day soon. I think you'll understand why we had to find a different place to live for a while."

Do We Have to Move?

David took Henk to the synagogue every Saturday morning. When they got there they put on little round caps. David put a shawl over his shoulders. They sat down with other families. A man read out loud from a book in front of the room. David said the man was the rabbi. David and the other people read with him. Even some boys read. Henk couldn't understand anything. Would it be hard to learn Hebrew?

Henk looked around the big room. The ceiling was very high up. Everyone sat on wooden benches. Many benches were empty and some broken ones were piled up in back of the room. There were eight big windows. Seven had wooden boards over them. But one was beautiful. It was made of red, blue, and yellow glass shaped like a star. The sun shone through it and made red, blue, and yellow designs on the wall. Henk wished he could stand in that bright colored light.

One Saturday morning David said, "I want to stop at our house today on the way home. We won't stay long."

They crossed the street to the house David had pointed out. Inside Henk couldn't see much at first. Wooden boards covered these windows, too. Only skinny slits of light sneaked in around the boards.

"These rooms were used as offices for the German commanders," David said.

Henk's footsteps echoed loudly as he slowly walked around on the bare floors of these dusty, empty rooms.

"Posters and signs must have hung over those light places on the walls," David explained. "That large rectangle over the desk was probably where a German flag hung."

The small German flags Henk had seen on trucks were red with a white circle in the middle. In the white circle was a bent black cross. He tried to imagine a very large one of these flags hanging in this room. He shivered.

"I think the German soldiers left the house in a

hurry, but first they threw the furniture around so no-body else could use it. They threw some of it out of the windows," David said.

"Was it your furniture?" Henk asked.

"Yes," David answered. "We had to leave all of our furniture in the house when we left. We hoped the neighbors would think that we had just gone away for a few days."

"Did the soldiers sleep in your beds?"

"Yes, they slept in our beds, Benjamin, but we won't go upstairs today, because the steps are not safe. The officers lived in our bedrooms. They kept some prisoners there, too."

"I don't think I want to live here. Why don't we stay in the apartment?" Henk asked David.

"Because this is our home, Benjamin. The work-men will make the house look like our home again. They will fix the walls and floors. You and I can come here every Saturday and see what they have done dur-ing the week." David sounded very cheerful. "And after they fix the stairs we will go up and look at your room! Now let's hurry home. Your mother will wonder where we are!"

21

Moving Day

"How will we get the boxes and furniture to the house?" Henk asked David. "Can we get a truck?"

"I wish we could, Benjamin, but there still is no gas for trucks. The German soldiers used all the gas in Holland for their tanks during the war. It will be a few months before we have fuel for trucks in Apelhem. But I have figured out a way to move our things. I think you'll agree it's a good idea, but I won't tell you what it is. It will be a surprise."

The workmen had hammered, plastered, and painted the house for weeks. At the apartment David and Elsbet had been packing books, clothes, and dishes into boxes. The front room looked just as it did the first time Henk walked in—full of boxes.

On the morning of moving day Henk played with Carl, so he wouldn't get in the way. Carl was crawling now.

The window of the front room was open because it was a warm day. Henk heard a farmer's cart stop in front of the building. He ran over and looked out like he always did. But this time he saw what he had been looking for!

"It's Papa. It's Pieter and Miep, too! What are they doing here? Are they going to help us move?"

"That's right, Benjamin," said David. "That's my surprise. I saw Paul Staal in the bank a few weeks ago. He offered to help us move. I knew you would want me to say yes."

Henk stuck his head way out the window. "Papa, look up—it's me, Henk! Miep, Pieter, look at me!"

Pieter jumped out of the cart, looked up, and waved. "Henk, come down! Let's see if you got any bigger!" he shouted.

Henk ran down the steps and right into Papa's arms. Papa held him very tight. It felt good to be held by Papa again.

After a few minutes Papa said, "I think you grew

two inches, Henk. Look, your head is almost up to my chest now! Stand back. Let me look at you."

Henk saw tears in Papa's eyes.

"I wish Mama could be here to see how big and healthy you look, but Tante Anna is sick. She couldn't leave her alone today."

Finally, Henk let go of Papa's hand and ran to Pieter. "I missed you, Pieter. But I have some friends now. We go to school and the park together."

Then he ran over to the cart. "Miep, jump down. I want to show you my schoolbooks and my baby brother!"

Miep was still sitting on the straw. Something black was in her lap.

"Kootje! You brought Kootje!" Henk scrambled up into the cart. "Let me hold her."

"Be careful, Henk. She's never been away from the farm before. She's frightened by the noisy streets here. Papa told me to hold her until we get to your new house."

"You mean I can keep her?" Henk asked. He stroked the top of the kitten's head. Then he put his cheek down on her soft fur.

"Of course you can! Papa told me your new house has a big yard. Kootje can play outside like she does on the farm."

David, Elsbet, Papa, and Pieter went up and down the steps carrying out boxes and furniture. They drove the loaded cart to the house, unloaded, and came back for more. Miep, Carl, and Henk played with Kootje in the apartment. Soon all the rooms were empty.

David came upstairs one more time. "Now it's time to lock up," he said. He picked up Carl. Miep and Henk, with Kootje in his arms, followed them down the stairs.

Henk watched David lock both doors. He remembered he had been afraid of this building with its locks and keys. He had also been afraid of this thin, pale man. Now he was used to David and not afraid of him, but he knew that he would always love Papa.

22

I Remember

At the house they all sat down and had some tea and milk and cake. Miep, Pieter, and Henk had to sit on boxes. There was not much furniture, but the house looked clean and pretty.

Miep ate her cake very slowly. "Mama sometimes bakes cakes now, too, when she can get some sugar," she told Henk.

Pieter finished his cake quickly. He went outside into the yard. Henk took Miep upstairs to show her his room.

"It's very big, Henk," she said. "Will Carl sleep with you?"

"Yes," Henk answered. He didn't tell her that he was still afraid to sleep alone.

They walked through the other rooms together. Henk's shoes made an echoing sound. Miep was wearing heavy socks. She had left her wooden shoes near the front door next to Papa's and Pieter's. Henk wished that Mama's shoes were there, too. He wanted to hug Mama, too, and feel her soft arms around him again.

"Tell Mama I miss her and I still play with the sock doll. Does she think about me?" Henk asked Miep.

"She says it's too quiet in the house when Pieter and I are in school. She was very sad that she couldn't come with us today. She wants you to come to the farm to see her," Miep said.

When Papa, Miep, and Pieter had to leave, Elsbet gave Papa a piece of cake for Mama and a small bag of sugar. Elsbet told Papa that they would come to visit as soon as the buses started running again.

Henk hoped that would be soon. He knew that it would only be a visit. His home was in Apelhem now with David and Elsbet. He waved good-bye as the cart rattled down the street. Kootje was on his lap.

Henk took Kootje out to the backyard to play. She stayed very close to him. "You still remember me,

Kootje, don't you?" Henk asked the cat. She rubbed against his leg.

The yard was big and there were thick bushes all around it. Suddenly, a rabbit jumped out from behind a tree. Kootje ran after it. Henk ran after Kootje. The rabbit disappeared into the bushes at the back of the yard. Kootje leaped in right after it.

"Kootje, Kootje, come back," Henk called. He ducked under a branch and into the bushes, too. He zigzagged through the bushes calling her name. Then he heard a "meow" and she was by his side again.

"Kootje, you're a naughty cat! You will get lost if you chase rabbits!"

As Henk bent over to pick her up, he saw a flat piece of wood sticking out from under some dry leaves. It had an eye painted on it! What could it be?

He brushed off the dirt and leaves. It was a wooden rocking horse, lying on its side. Faded patches of gray and white paint were on its body. A raggedy strap hung from one side of its mouth. Its tail was broken off, and one of its front legs was cracked. Two legs and one of the rockers were stuck in the hard ground.

"I remember this rocking horse, Kootje! I used to

ride this rocking horse! It was gray with white spots and had a red strap that I held. I'll show it to Elsbet."

Henk tried to pull the horse out from under the bush. It wouldn't move.

"Mama," he yelled toward the house, "I found my toy horse. Mama! Come see!" He was standing in front of the bushes now.

Elsbet stepped quickly out of the kitchen door. She ran across the yard. Henk took her hand and led her into the bushes. "Look what I found, Mama!" he said. He pointed to the broken horse. "I remember this rocking horse! I played on this rocking horse. It was mine, wasn't it?"

She knelt down next to Henk. She looked deep into his eyes. "Yes, Benjamin, it was yours, my son. It was yours!"

Her arm was around Henk's waist. She was holding him very close to her. Henk saw tears in her eyes. He put his arms around her neck.

"Mama, I think I remember you, too," Henk whispered to her. "You made the horse rock while I rode it."

She nodded her head. "Yes, I did, Benjamin."

"And I remember that I sat on your lap when you read to me *George of the Rebel Club*."

"You always loved that book!"

"And I remember that you held my hand when we walked home from the park after the soldier scared me."

She nodded again. "Yes."

"I remember you helped me put on my coat with the yellow star."

"Yes, Benjamin, I helped you put on your coat with the yellow star. Do you also remember your papa?" she asked.

"Yes." Henk looked down. "My papa put me in the cart to visit the farm. I cried when he didn't come back for me."

She picked up Henk's chin and kissed his cheek. "But now we are together again, Benjamin. Your papa did what he had to do. We are alive. We are safe. We are together again and we have Carl. Let's call Papa. Maybe he can fix that old rocking horse."

Henk and Elsbet stood up and walked toward the back door. He took her hand again and looked up at her face.

"Then I'll rock the little horse for my brother, Carl!"

Epilogue

When the Soldiers Were Gone is based on a true story. The real Benjamin spent the years from 1942 to 1945, during the German occupation of Holland, living on a farm near Hengelo, Holland, as a member of that Christian farm family. He was totally surprised to find out, after the war, that he had other parents, and he was very upset to learn he would have to leave the farm family he loved to live with "strangers."

Gradually Benjamin came to accept his real parents. He grew up happily in their Jewish home with his two brothers, one of whom was really his cousin. As he grew older he learned much about how his parents had managed to stay alive during the war, but, to this day, his mother finds those years painful to talk about.

"Papa" and "Mama" hid and helped many Dutch Jews besides Benjamin. "Papa" was awarded the *Ridde Kruis*, Knight's Cross, by Queen Beatrix of Holland, and he was listed in the official record of Dutch war heroes of World War II for his courage in hiding and protecting Jews.

As an adult, Benjamin emigrated to Canada, where he lived for several years and then emigrated to the United States. He now lives with his wife and two children in upstate New York.

He returns to Holland a few times a year to visit his mother, who still lives in Hengelo. One of his brothers lives in Canada, the other in Spain. His real father died. He also visits with the children of the farm family whenever he is in Holland. "Mama" and "Papa" are no longer living.